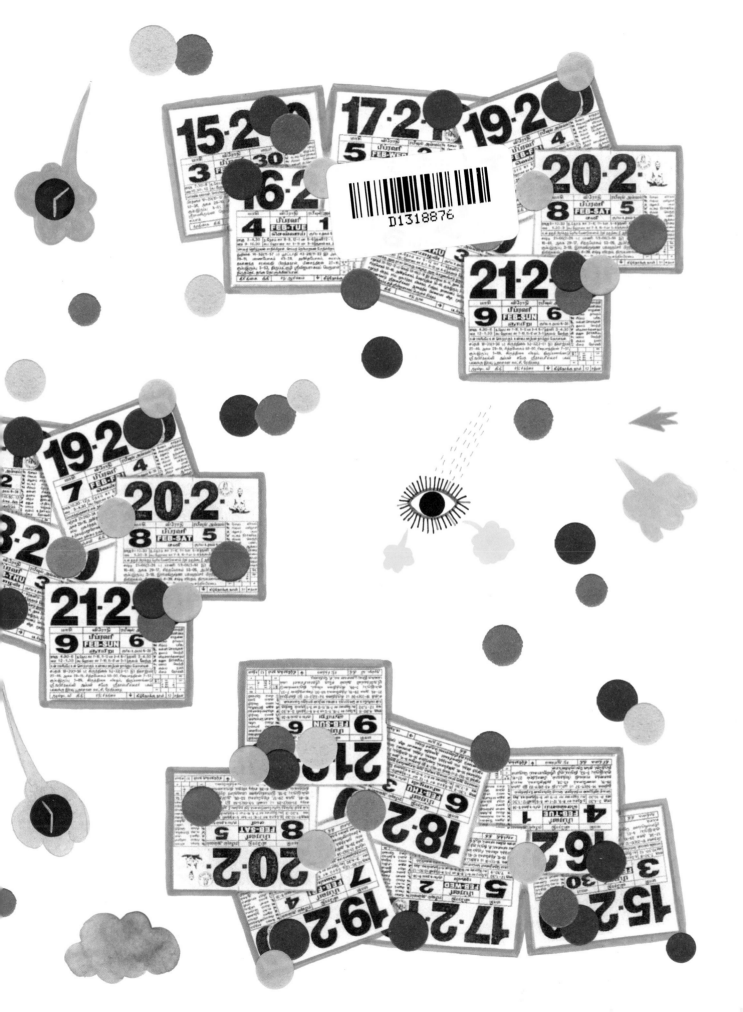

D1318876

Excuses *Excuses*

Marion Public Library
1095 6th Avenue
Marion, IA 52302-3428
(319) 377-3412

Text Anushka Ravishankar

Art Gabrielle Manglou

On Monday Neel decided
He'd be in time for school

On Tuesday he decided
He'd obey every rule

On Wednesday he decided
To be a helpful son

On Thursday he decided
To get all his homework done

On Friday he decided
To be sociable and good

On Saturday he decided
To do everything he should

On Sunday he decided
That he would mend his ways

Then suddenly he realized
That he'd run out of days.

Marion Public Library
1095 6th Avenue
Marion, IA 52302-3428
(319) 377-3412

MONDAY

Late again! What is it now?
Chased by a lion? Kicked by a cow?

I had an early dinner
I went to bed at eight
I set the clock for five because
I didn't want to be late—

I'd wake up early
Brush my teeth,
Wash my face
Rinse my feet
Have my breakfast
Nice and slow
Pack my bag
And off I'd go!!

BUT-

At night my clock began to tick
In an anti-clockwise way

And by the time I woke up
It was noon, of yesterday.

TUESDAY

No socks with your shoes?
What's your excuse?

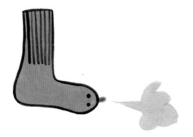

I was on my way to school
My shoes were polished bright
My uniform was starched, Sir
My socks were clean and white.

But suddenly I saw a crowd
Around an elephant
Which had stopped the traffic, it
Looked scared and hesitant.

A policeman was whistling
Cars were honking, too
People shouted, '*Cluck!*' and '*Coo!*'
And '**Scat!**' and '**Hiss!**' and '**SHOO!**'

I knew exactly what to do
To soothe the creature's fears
I went up there and stuffed my socks
Into its flapping ears.

The elephant went away
The crowd yelled, 'Hurray!'

And that is why I have no socks,
Only shoes, today.

WEDNESDAY

Where's the bread?
You brought a dog instead?

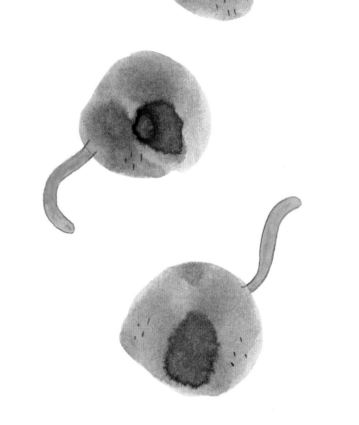

I went to buy bread just as you said
I was going into the store
When I saw a light brown dog
Just outside the door.

He looked at me with a piercing stare
I looked into his eyes
I remember nothing else,
I think I was hypnotized.

I don't know how I got back here,
And so, therefore, you see,

I didn't bring the dog back home —
He brought me.

THURSDAY

What's this wet and soggy thing?
Where's the homework I told you to bring?

My homework was done completely
I added, divided, I found out the square.
I wrote every sum down neatly
I finished it all, I promise, I swear!

Then, to my dismay, my homework hopped away.

And even though I shouted
'Come back here, come back!'
It leapt out of the window
And scooted down the track.

I chased it through the market
It jumped the traffic light
It hopped across the road without
Looking left or right.

'Such uncouth behaviour!'
Sniffed a granny with a wig
'Your homework has the manners
Of a badly brought up pig.'

It hopped into a pond
Saying, 'Ribit!' like a froggy

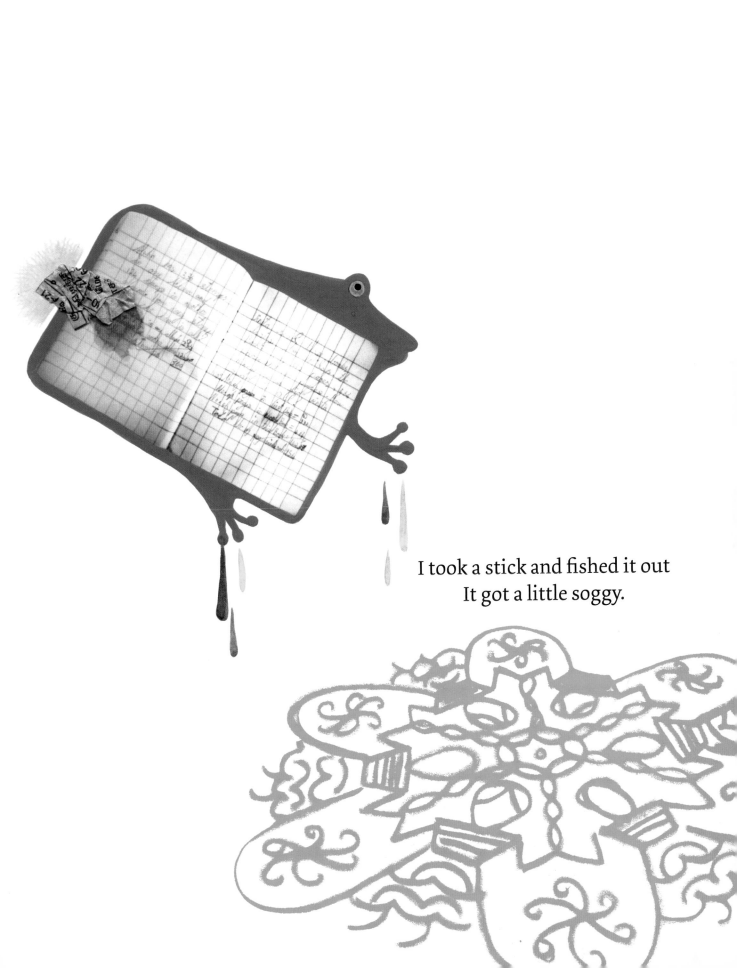

I took a stick and fished it out
It got a little soggy.

FRIDAY

Did you make Aunty go away?
What did you do? What did you say?

I was being nice and friendly
I was trying to be good
I was making conversation
Just as you said I should.

Her eyebrows were both missing
It gave me quite a scare
She had two inky arches
Instead of eyebrow hair.

So I asked her most politely,
'Where did your eyebrows go?
Did they slip away silently?
Or did they let you know?

Did you recently misplace them?
Have they been gone for long?'

'So rude!' she said, and stomped away
What did I do wrong?

SATURDAY

Water, water everywhere!
What have you been doing there?

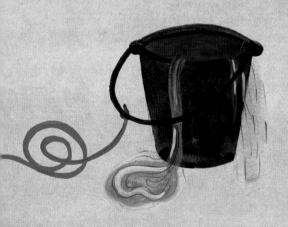

Clean your room, you always say
Sort it dust it scrub it
Wash it wipe it rub it
Clear it sweep it swab it
Soak it drench it daub it
Douse it rinse it spin it
Throw out the rubbish in it.

So I opened up the spout
And let the water out
Swish swosh slish slosh
I zoomed with a broom around the room.

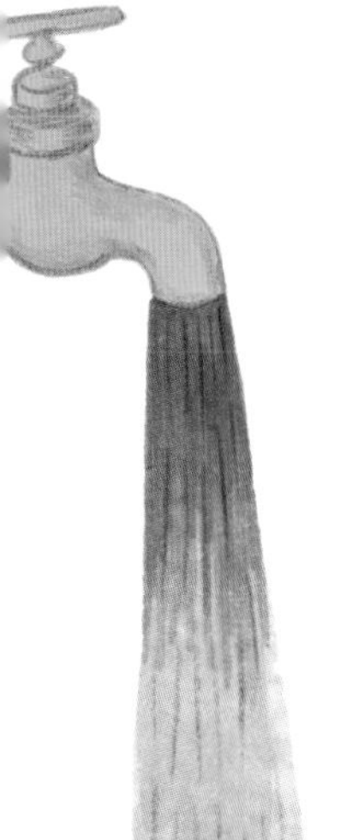

I know it's wet and sloppy,
but here's a happy thought:
You could come in and have a swim
The day is rather hot.

I hope you've learnt your lesson, son ...
Eeeeeeeeek! Now what have you done!!!

A day in the corner
That's what I got
A day to be sorry,
To spend with the thought
Of what I had done
And what I had not.

It was so boring
To sit on a chair
And not be allowed
To go anywhere.
It's Sunday today!
It's not at all fair!

I'd no one to talk to
Nothing to do
So I slept and I dreamed
Of an artist who drew
On a wall. When I woke up
The dream had come true!

I looked for the artist—
I think it's a shame
That he's done this painting
And not signed his name.

Try as Neel might
Things never went right
And though he explained how he really tried,
What deeply grieved him
Was no one believed him.

Excuses! Excuses! Excuses! they cried.

But Neel told himself,
There's no cause for sorrow,
I'll start once again—
It's a new week tomorrow!

Excuses, Excuses!
Copyright © Tara Books Pvt. Ltd. 2011

For the text:
Anushka Ravishankar

For the illustrations:
Gabrielle Manglou

For this edition:
Tara Books, India, *tarabooks.com*
and Tara Publishing Ltd., UK, *tarabooks.com/uk*

Design: Rathna Ramanathan, minus 9 Design and Nia Murphy
Production: C. Arumugam
Printed in China through Asia Pacific Offset

All rights reserved. No part of this book may be reproduced in any form,
without the prior written permission of the publisher.

ISBN: 978-93-80340-12-8

A big thank you to our model **Neel Hariharan**, whose histrionics
inspired us to greater heights of wackiness.